The Orphan Rescue

The Orphan Rescue

by Anne Dublin
illustrated by Qin Leng

Second Story Press

Library and Archives Canada Cataloguing in Publication

Dublin, Anne
The orphan rescue / by Anne Dublin.

ISBN 978-1-897187-81-4

I. Title.

PS8557.U233O76 2010   jC813'.6   C2010-904361-8

Edited by Sarah Swartz
Copyedited by Kathryn White
Designed by Melissa Kaita
Cover and illustrations by Qin Leng

Printed and bound in Canada

The author gratefully acknowledges the support of the Ontario Arts Council.

*Second Story Press gratefully acknowledges the support of the Ontario Arts Council and
the Canada Council for the Arts for our publishing program. We acknowledge
the financial support of the Government of Canada through the Book
Publishing Industry Development Program.*

 ONTARIO ARTS COUNCIL
CONSEIL DES ARTS DE L'ONTARIO

 Canada Council   Conseil des Arts
for the Arts   du Canada

Published by
SECOND STORY PRESS
20 Maud Street, Suite 401
Toronto, ON M5V 2M5
www.secondstorypress.ca

Contents

PROLOGUE...1

CHAPTER 1 The Family 7

CHAPTER 2 Hard Decisions....................................15

CHAPTER 3 At the Orphanage 25

CHAPTER 4 Ben...32

CHAPTER 5 The Visit 41

CHAPTER 6 Mr. Sharf 48

CHAPTER 7 The Scavenger....................................58

CHAPTER 8 Unexpected Help 67

CHAPTER 9 At the Restaurant 74

CHAPTER 10 The Rescue..83

CHAPTER 11 Miriam's Plan 87

CHAPTER 12 Almost Home 93

CHAPTER 13 Miriam in Trouble 99

CHAPTER 14 The Truth About Mr. Reznitsky 106

CHAPTER 15 The End Is the Beginning...................114

AFTERWORD FROM THE AUTHOR 121

ACKNOWLEDGMENTS..123

Poland, 1937

The city of Sosnowiec

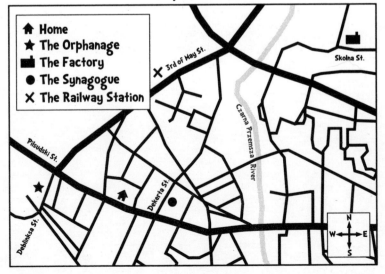

PROLOGUE
Sosnowiec, Poland

May 1937

"There it is," Grandfather said as he pointed to the large, red brick building. Black letters on a sign above the wrought iron gate announced "The Jewish Orphanage of Sosnowiec."

Grandfather pulled the rope beside the gate. A bell clanged loudly and made Miriam jump. The little piece of dry bread she had eaten for breakfast lay heavy in her stomach. Her brother David's lips were trembling.

A tall, thin man walked toward the gate. His bald head, beady eyes, and long pointed nose made him look like a vulture. "Mr. Goldstein," the man said, in

a cold voice. "I have been expecting you."

Grandfather nodded and shook the man's hand. "Children, this is Mr. Reznitsky, the director of the orphanage," he said. He put his hand on David's shoulder. "And this is my grandson, David, and his sister, Miriam."

Mr. Reznitsky stared up and down at David. Then he opened the heavy gate. "Please come in."

They walked along the path that led from the gate to the front door. At the side of the building, some boys and girls were weeding a vegetable garden or hanging clothes on lines stretched between poles. The boys wore striped shirts and navy blue pants. The girls wore white blouses and navy skirts.

The children stared at the newcomers. Miriam felt her face grow red.

"Our orphans go to their lessons or to their workshops in the morning," Mr. Reznitsky said. "In the afternoon they do chores to help keep this place running."

"Grandfather, I don't want to stay here!" David cried as he tugged on Grandfather's hand. "I don't like it here. Take me home!" Tears flowed down his cheeks and snot ran from his nose. He wiped his face with his sleeve.

"David, don't be afraid," Grandfather said as he patted David's head. Mr. Reznitsky ignored David's cries.

I'd be afraid, too, if I were left here in the orphanage, thought Miriam. *I want to leave this place and go back home. Home—where I know every piece of furniture, every dish in the cupboard.*

"David, listen," Miriam said. "Here's my special handkerchief. Blow your nose."

"On your handkerchief? Really?" David asked in a trembling voice.

Miriam nodded. "Give it a good blow."

David blew his nose. All the while, he stared at Miriam, as if she were about to disappear.

"You know what?" Miriam said. "If you stop crying, you can keep it."

David nodded. "I'll...I'll try." He hiccupped several times, wiped his tears, and stuffed the handkerchief into his pocket.

"Here we are," said Mr. Reznitsky. "Come into my office."

Miriam had never seen such a beautiful room. Hundreds of books sat on shelves that went from the floor to the ceiling. Children's artwork was tacked on a large cork board. A large oak desk with a comfortable leather chair stood in the center of the room. Near one bookcase, a canary chirped inside a wire cage.

"David, I give you permission to sit at that table near my desk," Mr. Reznitsky said. "Here are some colored pencils." He tried to be pleasant to the boy. "Your grandfather told me you like to draw."

"I'll draw with him," Miriam offered.

Who will draw with David after we leave? Miriam wondered. The grownups spoke in low voices while Miriam sat drawing beside her brother.

After a few minutes, Grandfather stood up. He looked upset and shaken. Softly he said, "Miriam, it is time. David, dear boy, you must be brave." He bent down to kiss David on the head.

Miriam stood up quickly and grabbed one of

Grandfather's hands. *I won't let Grandfather leave me behind,* she thought.

"Be a good boy," Grandfather whispered.

"Don't go!" David wailed. "Grandfather! Miriam!"

"David, they must leave now," said Mr. Reznitsky. "Don't be a crybaby. They will come back to see you soon."

David didn't answer. He clung to Grandfather. They hugged each other tightly. Miriam joined them in a three-way hug. Each of them tried hard not to cry.

Mr. Reznitsky interrupted them. "Now I will walk with you to the gate," he said to Grandfather. He looked at David and said sternly, "You stay here."

As she went out the door, Miriam glanced back at David one more time. The gate closed behind them with a dull, heavy clang.

CHAPTER 1
The Family

It wasn't always like this, Miriam thought as she walked home with Grandfather. *We were a family once—Mama and Papa, David and me, Grandfather and Grandmother.*

Miriam, David, and their parents had lived in three rooms in the center of the Jewish neighborhood in Sosnowiec.

Forty years ago, Sosnowiec was a small town. It had grown into a city because of the coal mines and factories. People looking for jobs poured in from the surrounding towns and villages. From this corner in southwest Poland, people could travel south to Austria, west to Germany, or east to Russia.

Papa was a watchmaker. Miriam loved to sit on the high stool next to his workbench as she watched his nimble fingers at work.

"Now this is a fine watch," Papa would say, pointing with his thin tweezers at a gold watch from Switzerland. "I will make it run again, to the second." He took the watch apart. Then he looked at the tiny parts through his magnifying eyepiece. By the time he finished, it worked better than new.

It was a difficult time for the family. They didn't have much money, but they were together and they were happy. Like many other people in Poland, they made do with the little they had. "People don't bring their watches and clocks for me to fix anymore," Papa said. "They must think that correct time is a luxury." He paused. "And it is, compared to having something to eat."

It was the early 1930s and Poland was in the Great Depression, like the rest of the world. The Great Depression meant that there were many people out of work.

Then, five winters ago, an epidemic of typhus killed many people in Sosnowiec. Papa was one of its victims.

When Papa died, Miriam was seven years old and David only two. Miriam remembered Mama's torn dress, the mirror covered with a dark cloth, the low boxes they had sat on—as was the Jewish custom for mourning. Their neighbors had come every day to say *kaddish*, the mourners' prayer.

After thirty days of mourning, Mama found a job in a dressmaking shop. When she came home from work, she would sit by the window in summer or by the light of the kerosene lamp during the long, dark winter evenings.

Mama stopped smiling after Papa died. Miriam wondered if something had died inside Mama, too. At night Miriam could hear Mama crying beside her in the bed. Miriam always tried to lie still so that Mama didn't know she was listening.

Now Miriam's memories of Papa were like faded letters in an old book. She sometimes gazed at the wedding photo of Mama and Papa hanging on the wall. Mama was very beautiful in the picture. She sat on a hard-backed chair, while Papa stood behind her, his hand resting on her shoulder. They both seemed so young and hopeful.

As the years passed, things had gotten worse for the family. Sometimes there wasn't enough money for food or coal for the stove. All they had to eat was thin potato soup and a piece of bread. Miriam's tummy often rumbled with hunger, even after supper. David's face was pale and he caught bad colds in the winter.

Mama sold her pearl earrings and her gold wedding band. Papa's tools for fixing watches were sold to a young man who had been Papa's apprentice. Yet they still didn't have enough money. Finally they could no longer pay the rent. They had to leave their rooms.

Mama, Miriam, and David moved in with Grandmother and Grandfather. The five of them then lived in two rooms on Pilsudski Street where Grandfather had his locksmith shop with the sign of a lock and key over the front door.

It was a mixed blessing to live with Grandmother and Grandfather. It was nice to be together, but there was not much space. It was freezing in winter and blistering hot in summer. Paint was peeling from the walls, and the wood floor was uneven and full of splinters.

The back room served as kitchen, living-room, and bedroom combined. The walls were bare except for a calendar and two wedding photos. Long ago, books had filled another shelf—Hebrew prayer books for festivals and every day, books of stories and legends from the Bible, and even a few Yiddish books written for women. But now the books were gone—sold to the peddler for a few pennies. Two beds were squeezed together against the wall on one side of the room. A wooden table and four chairs stood on the opposite side. A coal stove leaned against the third wall.

Two buckets—one for clean water and the other for dirty—sat on a small bench next to the cupboard where Grandmother kept the dishes. There was no money to buy water from the water carrier.

Mama or Miriam had to walk three blocks to get water from the public pump. They shared the outhouse with three other families. It was smelly and filled with spiders. Miriam tried to hold her nose every time she had to go.

The courtyard was surrounded on all sides by four-storey buildings where people lived and worked. Windows looked out on the courtyard. The outhouse was on the side where people kept their garbage cans. On the other side, Grandfather had built a little shed for Mottele, the goat. Grandmother took care of the goat for Mrs. Krangle, the butcher's wife. Grandmother often said the goat reminded her of the farm where she had grown up.

Mottele was brown except for a white line that ran from the tip of his nose up to his forehead. He had four white hooves, which Miriam imagined were high boots he put on every morning to protect his shapely feet. Miriam often thought that Mottele didn't belong here, in this city of hard stones and bricks, of coal smoke and damp rain.

Miriam remembered her last birthday, when everyone sat around the kitchen table. She had already opened most of her presents. There were chocolates from Grandfather, a pair of socks from Grandmother, and a painting from David.

"For your twelfth birthday," Mama said, handing Miriam a small package wrapped in blue tissue. "I made a special present for you."

"What, Mama?" Miriam said.

"Open it!" said David.

Miriam tore the tissue as slowly as she could. Inside was a white cotton handkerchief. It was embroidered in one corner with purple violets and dark green leaves.

"Oh, Mama!" Miriam cried. "I love it! I'll keep it always!"

Mama gave Miriam a rare smile. "I'm glad you like it."

"Now you have a handkerchief like a fancy lady," said Grandmother.

"Even a lady needs to blow her nose," said Grandfather.

"You're not going to give me one of those for *my* birthday, are you Mama?" said David.

"Not that you'd use it!" said Miriam, nudging her brother. "You'd rather use your sleeve."

"Well, it's always there when I need it," said David, grinning.

Six months ago, Mama had lost her job at the dress shop. She had to go door-to-door selling needles, buttons, and thread. One day, she stayed out in the cold rain too long and caught pneumonia.

"Take care of David," Mama had whispered. "Promise me."

"I will, Mama," said Miriam. "I promise."

After three days, Mama had died. Miriam knew that her world would never be the same again.

CHAPTER 2
Hard Decisions

From early morning until late at night, Grandfather used to sit on a stool behind his workbench in the front room, which smelled of oil and metal. But soon after Mama died, he had to stop working. Grandfather had accidentally dropped a very heavy box on his right hand. Three fingers were broken and didn't mend. Since then, Grandfather had not been able to do any work as a locksmith.

The only money that came in was from Grandmother's knitting. She knit new sweaters from the wool of old sweaters and tried to sell them in the market. But she was often ill and couldn't always work.

Then came one of the worst days in Miriam's life. She was reading a book in the courtyard. The sun was warm; the birds were singing. She felt almost happy for the first time since Mama had died.

Grandfather walked out to the courtyard and sat down beside Miriam on an old wooden box. He wiped his forehead with his handkerchief. "Dear girl, you know how hard things have been lately?"

Miriam put her finger in the book so she wouldn't lose her place. "Yes."

"We don't know where the next *groshen* will come from to buy food." He cleared his throat. "So your grandmother and I have decided that—"

"What?"

Grandfather swallowed hard. "We have decided that you must leave school and go to work."

"No!" cried Miriam. "I love school!" She could feel her throat getting tight and tears coming to her eyes. "I want to be a teacher when I grow up!"

Grandfather shook his head and pursed his lips. "I know. But it is impossible now." He put his arm around Miriam's shoulders, but she shook it off. "This Monday, you will start working at Mr. Krangle's butcher shop."

"Please, Grandfather," Miriam begged. "Please don't make me!"

Grandfather looked down at the ground. "We need your help to earn some money," he said. "The world is not a kind place for our family."

Miriam stood up and rushed inside.

Grandmother was unraveling the wool from an old sweater. Her eyes were red, and she looked as if she had been crying. She gave a little cough and then called to Miriam. Grandmother often coughed when she tried to speak, but there was no money for doctors to find out why.

"Miriam?" she called again.

But Miriam ignored her and plopped down on the bed.

Grandfather followed Miriam and sat down beside her. "There's more to tell you," he said.

Miriam looked up at him with a tearstained face. "What more can there be?"

"David must go to the orphanage," Grandfather said.

"The orphanage? What do you mean?" cried Miriam.

"We must send him to the orphanage," Grandfather repeated in a miserable voice.

"Where he'll be better taken care of," said Grandmother.

"No! You can't send him away!" Miriam jumped up from the bed and began to pace the narrow space between the table and the beds. "I don't care if we're the poorest Jews in the city!" she cried. "I don't care if we're the poorest people in the whole world! We need to stay together. How can you be so mean to us?"

Grandmother stopped unraveling the wool and crossed her arms. "We are just as unhappy about this as you are," she said. "But we can no longer provide for the two of you."

Miriam knew she was being rude and should respect her elders. But today she could not. Grownups were supposed to know what to do. They were supposed to take care of their children. They were supposed to give them food, clothing, an education. The grownups in her family couldn't do any of those things! First her parents had died. Now her grandparents had decided to take her out of school and send her brother away.

"The child is right to be angry," Grandfather said, shaking his head in despair. "I am angry, too."

Miriam looked at her grandfather. He was the kindest man she had ever known. He never raised his voice and, before their troubles, always had a smile on his face. Miriam remembered when she used to sit on Grandfather's lap. She loved the scratchy feel of his wool sweater and his salty breath from the herring and onions he liked to eat.

Miriam sat down on a kitchen chair. She put her chin in her hands and stared at the worn wooden floor. She could feel the tears welling up in her eyes, but she didn't bother to wipe them away. Soon her cheeks, her chin, even her hair were wet.

"Miriam! Look what I found!" shouted David, slamming the door behind him and storming into the room.

"Don't slam the door," said Grandmother in a flat voice.

Miriam hid her face in her hands. She couldn't bear to pretend that everything was fine.

David stared at Grandmother and Grandfather, then at Miriam. "Why isn't anyone talking?" he asked.

He walked over to Miriam and shook her shoulder. "Miriam, look!" David leaned closer to her and yelled in her ear, "Miriam!" Then he whispered softly, "Look what I found."

Miriam glanced up. A tiny nose and eyes like shiny black beads stared back at her. A gray kitten was tucked into David's half-open jacket. The kitten began to meow.

Grandmother turned David around to face her. "Don't hide it," she said, wagging her finger at her grandson. "It's a cat."

"It's just a *little* cat," said David, pushing the kitten's head back into his jacket. But its head kept poking out as if its neck were on a spring.

"Outside!" said Grandmother, pointing toward the door.

"Please," David said. His eyes filled with tears. "Please let me keep it."

"Little cats grow into big ones," said Grandfather, shaking his head. "Besides—"

"He was starving in the alley," David whined.

"And we're starving in our own home," muttered Grandfather. "There's not even enough food for us. And no extra food for a kitten."

"I'm sorry, David. You must put the cat outside," Grandmother said more kindly. She pushed David's hair out of his eyes.

David brushed her hand away. He slammed the door as he left the room. The clock on the wall ticked loudly.

After a few minutes, David came back. His face was dirty and streaked with tears. "I did what you told me to do," he said.

"Sit down, David," said Grandfather. "There is something we need to talk about."

"I won't go!" David shouted.

"David, you are seven years old now," said Grandfather.

"Almost eight," said David, raising his chin.

"Yes, almost eight." Grandfather paused. "Try to understand that we are doing this because we have no other choice."

"At the orphanage," Grandmother said, her voice shaking, "you will have good food to eat and clothes to wear. You will have other children to play with."

"I don't care!" David cried. "I want to stay here!"

"You will see," Grandfather said. "Everything will be fine. You'll be able to go to school. And when you're older, they will teach you a trade."

David pointed at Miriam. "She's older," he said. "Why can't she go instead of me?"

Grandmother shook her head. "They won't take her."

Miriam had a sick feeling in her stomach. "I didn't know you'd asked about me, too."

"Why won't they?" asked David.

"Miriam's too old. Twelve already," Grandfather said.

"Don't talk about me like I'm not here," said Miriam.

"If Miriam doesn't have to go, I won't either!" David shouted.

"It's just for a little while," said Grandmother.

"Until I can work again," added Grandfather.

"I don't believe you!" cried David. "You'll send me there and then you'll forget all about me!"

"We could never forget about you," said Grandmother, bursting into tears. "You are our grandson, and we love you."

"Always remember, David," Grandfather said, wagging his finger. "You were born into this family. You were not born from a stone. And we will stay a family no matter where you are living." He cleared his throat. "Every Saturday we will visit you there, or you will visit us here."

Tears welled up in David's eyes, and his voice became softer. "You promise?"

"We promise," said Grandmother.

David sat up straighter. "You said I'll get good food?" he asked.

Grandmother nodded.

"And they'll give me new clothes and shoes?"

Grandfather nodded.

"I'll try it then," he said, his lips trembling.

"My dear boy," said Grandfather with tears in his eyes. "I promise we'll come to see you on the Sabbath right after the service."

CHAPTER 3
At the Orphanage

David's eyes followed Grandfather and Miriam as they walked out the door. He glanced about Mr. Reznitsky's office, looked at the bulletin board, and sat down at the little table.

David wasn't sure he liked Mr. Reznitsky—or trusted him. On the way here, Grandfather had said, "In this world, there are good people and bad people." He paused. "This orphanage was built by good people in the Jewish community."

"Rich good people?" David asked.

"What do you think?" said Miriam. "Rich bad people?"

David stuck out his tongue. "There must be some of those."

"Of course there are," said Grandfather. "But the people who are in charge of the orphanage do it because it's a *mitzvah*, a good deed. They help the poor and needy."

"That's us," said Miriam, putting her arm around David's shoulders. "Poor and needy."

"Needy and poor," David said.

David stared into space for a while and then picked up a pencil. He drew a big house with lots of windows; a sun shining on a garden filled with flowers. Then he added a thin gray cat sitting on the sidewalk. He felt like that stray kitten, unwanted, put out on the street.

It's not a bad picture, David thought when he finished. *But I'll never be able to show it to Miriam or Grandmother.* He put his head on his arms and began to sob.

The door opened and Mr. Reznitsky walked back into the room. Now his beady eyes focused on

David. "David, tell me about your picture," he said, pretending interest.

I won't answer, thought David.

"Where did you learn to draw like that?"

David shrugged. He didn't like how Mr. Reznitsky leaned over him. He felt as though he couldn't breathe.

Mr. Reznitsky pulled up a little chair and sat down beside David. "You draw very well," he said. "Tell me, David. I would really like to know."

David swallowed hard. "Sometimes Grandmother gave me a piece of charcoal or a pencil." He rolled the pencil back and forth on the desk. "Or I would draw with a stick in the dirt outside."

"Let's put your drawing up on the board with the others. Would you like that?" asked Mr. Reznitsky with a fake smile.

"I guess so." David sniffed. "But could I have it back if I want?" *When I leave here,* he thought. *When I go back home.*

Mr. Reznitsky nodded. "Tell me, David, do you know how to write your name?"

David wiped his nose with the back of his hand. Then he remembered Miriam's handkerchief and took it out of his pocket. It smelled of Grandmother's soap, and he almost started to cry again. He swallowed hard, blew his nose, and put the handkerchief back into his pocket.

"Miriam showed me how to write my name when I was little," David said. He printed his name carefully on a corner of the drawing.

Mr. Reznitsky took some thumbtacks from a drawer in his desk. He pressed David's picture onto the bulletin board. "Now put your pencil down. You need to get settled in your new home," he said less patiently.

This isn't my home, David thought. *It will never be.*

Mr. Reznitsky led David out of his office and along the corridor. He opened a door that said "Staff Room."

"Joshua, please come here."

A tall young man came out of the room. His head bobbed on his long neck as if it wasn't fastened on quite right. "Yes, Mr. Reznitsky?" he said.

"Joshua, this is David Goldstein, our new boy," said Mr. Reznitsky.

"Hello, David," said Joshua.

"Joshua will be your counselor while you are here," said Mr. Reznitsky. "I am sure you will get along just fine." He glanced at his watch and hurried away.

"Come along, David," said Joshua.

"Who made this orphanage?" David asked.

"It's not one 'who,' but lots of people."

"Huh?"

"A group of people from the Jewish community formed a committee. They raised the money and bought the building. Then they hired people to run it."

"Was Mr. Reznitsky hired by those people?"

"That's right." Joshua paused. "Did Mr. Reznitsky tell you that every kid must do work here?" he said.

David nodded.

"You'll start by helping in the kitchen." Joshua led David along the corridor and into a large kitchen.

A big stove stood between two long counters; a tall refrigerator, between two rows of brightly painted cupboards. A large porcelain sink with running water was set against another wall. Sunlight streamed in through a window above the sink.

"Hello, Joshua," said a young woman. She had dark, serious eyes and a broad, plain face. Curly red hair had escaped from under her kerchief and her forehead was beaded with sweat. She was stirring what smelled like borscht soup in a huge pot. "Who's that?" She pointed with a long wooden spoon at David.

"David is our new orphan," Joshua said. Then he turned to David and explained, "Bluma has been here about eight years now. She was one of the first orphans. And now she's our head cook."

Will I have to live here for the rest of my life, too? David wondered.

CHAPTER 4
Ben

A thin, wiry boy was standing in front of the sink filled with soapy water.

"Hello, Ben. How are you today?" asked Joshua.

"I'm tired of washing all these dishes," said Ben as he turned his head.

"Now, Ben, at least it's a *clean* job. Don't you like it more than working in the garden?"

Ben slapped the dishrag against the sink. "I don't like *any* of the jobs," he said. David stepped away from the growing puddle on the floor.

Joshua shook his head. "This is David," he said. "He's seven."

"Almost eight," said David.

"Kind of small, aren't you?" said Ben.

David blushed. People always said that about him.

"Ben will show you what to do," said Joshua. "I have to see how the other kids are doing. I'll see you soon at supper."

Ben took a dish towel from a hook and handed it to David. "Dry the dishes that are in the rack. Then put them on the counter." He peered at David and said, "Where are you from?"

"What?" said David.

"Where are you *from*? What city? What town?"

"Oh," said David. "From here."

"Where here?"

"Close by, here in Sosnowiec. My family is coming to visit me soon," he added quickly.

Ben stared at David. "If you've got a family, what are you doing here?" he asked.

David swallowed hard. "I don't have parents," he said.

"You still have a family though, don't you?" Ben

said. "I saw them when you came. I watch every new person who comes here."

"Yes, but—"

"Forget it," Ben snapped. "Get back to work."

A bell rang a few minutes later. Joshua came for David. "Time for supper," he said.

They walked into the adjoining dining room. It soon filled up with noisy children sitting on benches along the tables covered with oilcloth. Each of the six tables was supervised by a young adult. Later, David would find out they were either student teachers or former residents of the orphanage.

All the girls had short hair. Some of the boys' heads looked as if they had been shaved. *I hope it's not because of lice*, David thought. He had had lice last year, and the barber had shaved his head. Grandmother had washed his head with soap that stung.

"Sit here, David, at our table," motioned Joshua. "Come and meet the others."

David sat down next to a skinny boy with red

hair and freckles. He looked at David with mischievous blue eyes.

"Hello," said the boy. "My name is Sam. What's your name?"

"David."

"Where are you from?" Sam asked.

"From here," said David.

"Most of the kids are, too," said Sam. He pointed to his chest and shook his head. "Not me. I'm from—"

"The new boy isn't a real orphan," interrupted Ben, leaning over from the next table.

Sam raised his eyebrows. "What?"

"He's got family." Ben stared at David. "Which means he's not an orphan."

Sam shrugged. "So what?"

Mr. Reznitsky was sitting at a table at the front of the room. He soon stood up and rang a little bell. The room became quiet. "Boys and girls," he began, "we have a new member in our community." He looked in David's direction. "Stand up, David."

David slowly got to his feet. "This is David

Goldstein, who's seven years old. Now, children, we will say the blessing." Mr. Reznitsky paused. "David, you may sit down." Everyone laughed. David felt his face growing red.

One of the older boys made a blessing over the bread. Joshua sliced the rye bread and passed the plate around.

David took a bite of the bread and chewed slowly. Bluma and her helpers brought bowls filled with hot borscht soup. David couldn't remember the last time his grandmother made borscht as rich as this. He put his spoon down and stared at the soup. *How can I enjoy this when my family doesn't have enough to eat?* he wondered.

The aroma of the soup made his mouth water. He picked up his spoon and began to slurp the soup greedily.

"Hey David, are you inhaling the soup?" Sam teased. He laughed and slapped David on the back.

I hope Sam will be my friend, David thought. *It feels good to be laughing with another boy.*

After dinner, Joshua said, "Sam, can you help David get settled?"

"Sure," said Sam. "Let's go."

At the end of the hallway, Sam opened the door of a storeroom.

Piles of clothes and shoes were stacked on shelves reaching almost to the ceiling. "Here, here, and here," Sam said as he piled clothing into David's arms.

They walked up one flight of stairs and along a hallway until they came to a room with a sign that said "Boys Dormitory."

"You can have the bed next to mine," said Sam, pointing to an iron cot near the door. "That boy is gone."

David put his bag on a shelf above his bed. He smoothed out the gray woolen blanket and the freshly washed sheets.

"Where did he go?" David asked.

"He was adopted last week." Sam put his hand on David's arm. "Let's go to the sitting room."

They made their way to a room on the main floor.

Children were talking and laughing. David had to dodge their elbows and feet until he found a place to sit. Not one chair matched the other. Some children were reading. Others played chess, checkers, or dominos.

David saw a stack of paper and colored pencils on a small table. "Can I use these?" he asked.

"Sure," Sam said. He pulled an atlas down from a shelf crammed with books while David began to draw.

"One day," Sam said, sitting down beside David, "I'll be a rich merchant and travel all over the world. I'll sell expensive silks and jewels. People will rush to buy my goods. 'Sam, the merchant,' they will say, 'is the best in the country.'"

David drew an older version of Sam, with a double chin, grizzled red beard, and fat belly. A heavy gold watch hung from a chain on Sam's striped vest.

"Hey, not bad," said Sam. "You know, we have our own newspaper here. Maybe you can draw for it. Maybe you'll even become a world-famous artist! You'll paint portraits of all the ladies and gentlemen in Poland. Or France. Maybe even America!"

David shook his head. "No, I won't," he said. "I need a lot more practice. Besides, artists only get famous after they die." He pointed the pencil at Sam. "I'll need help from my rich merchant friend to support me."

"I'll be glad to be your wealthy friend." Sam grinned. "Then I'll be able to say I knew you when."

"When what?"

Sam elbowed David. "Uh-oh! Here comes trouble," he whispered.

Ben stood at the doorway, his hands in his pockets. He looked at everyone in the room, like a shark ready to swallow the smaller fish in his path.

He stalked over to David and glanced at the drawing. "So here's the kid who calls himself an orphan," he said.

"I…I don't," said David.

"Yeah, sure," said Ben. He shoved David on the shoulder and stalked away.

David choked back his tears. "Can't we tell Mr. Reznitsky that he's bullying me?"

"Are you kidding? And get in trouble for being a tattletale? Besides," Sam added, "Mr. Reznitsky is a coward."

"What do you mean?"

"You'll see," said Sam.

CHAPTER 5
The Visit

A week passed. And when the next Sabbath finally arrived, Miriam walked with Grandmother and Grandfather to the big synagogue on Dekerta Street. Grandmother leaned heavily on Miriam's shoulder as they climbed the stairs to the women's section. She had to stop several times to catch her breath.

"Grandmother," said Miriam. "Are you all right?"

"I'll be fine," said Grandmother, coughing.

The light from the stained-glass windows lit up the room with dancing colors of blues and greens, reds and yellows. Miriam peeked over the women's barrier and managed to find Grandfather among all the men and boys standing below. By habit, her eyes looked for David, who always played with the fringes on Grandfather's white prayer shawl. The men's prayer shawls were like the sails of a ship she had seen in her schoolbook. *I wish I could sail away to a happier place*, she thought.

She sat quietly amid the prayers and murmurs, the whispers and gossip of the women. But all she could think about was David. *We'll see him today*, she thought. *See him today. See him today.* The words kept repeating in her head, like the wheels of a train going round and round.

After the service was over, Grandmother said, "I'm not feeling well. I should not have come." She doubled over with a coughing fit and had trouble catching her breath. "I have to go home." She wiped her eyes with her shawl. "It breaks my heart, but I am just not strong enough to visit David today."

Miriam shivered when she saw the high brick wall in front of the orphanage. It reminded her of a prison. *Does David feel like a prisoner?* she wondered.

"Come, Miriam," said Grandfather, taking her hand gently. "Let's go inside."

They made their way into a large sitting room. People sat in small groups, talking in low voices. Miriam sat down on a hard chair and waited impatiently.

All at once, David raced into the room. He dashed over to where Grandfather and Miriam were sitting.

"You came!" he shouted, squeezing himself into the same chair as Grandfather.

Miriam felt the tears welling in her eyes. Until now, she hadn't known how much she missed David. David chattered away, telling them all about the orphanage and his new friend.

A few minutes later, a group of older children came into the room. They carried trays of cookies and lemonade. They placed them on tables around the room for the visitors. David stopped talking when he saw that Ben was one of the helpers.

Mr. Reznitsky entered the room and cleared his throat. "Ladies and gentlemen, boys and girls," he said in a haughty voice. "Welcome to visiting day."

For the next fifteen minutes, Mr. Reznitsky droned on about the work he was doing at the orphanage. Some of the adults began to doze; the children fidgeted and made faces behind his back.

At last, Mr. Reznitsky cleared his throat and said, "Now our helpers will serve refreshments. You may stay until three o'clock. At that time, visiting will be over."

Miriam had the feeling that someone was staring at her. She didn't want to turn her head to look, but she felt prickles up and down her spine. When the polite applause ended, she turned and saw a tall, thin boy looking at her. She felt herself blush when the boy picked up a tray and carried it toward them.

"Thank you, young man," said Grandfather, holding a glass in one hand and a poppy seed cookie in the other. "What's your name?"

"Ben."

"And how old are you?"

"Fourteen," Ben said.

"Have you been here long?"

Ben nodded. "Too long." He pressed his lips together and said, "I have to go now."

"Of course," said Grandfather. "Thank you, Ben."

Ben nodded and hurried away.

"A nice boy," said Grandfather.

"I don't like him," David whispered, glancing over his shoulder.

"Why not?" said Miriam.

"He says…he says I'm not an orphan," said David. "Because I have family."

Miriam put her arm around David's shoulder and hugged him tightly. "Maybe he's right," she said.

"What do you mean?"

"As long as you've got me, you're not an orphan!" she said.

David wiped his nose on his sleeve.

"David!" said Miriam.

"Oops!" He took out his handkerchief and blew into it loudly.

"You sound like a goose!" said Miriam.

After their visit, Miriam walked home with Grandfather. She kept thinking about David and what she had seen at the orphanage. Grandfather had to pull her hand or she would have stepped into a pile of steaming horse dung.

When they came home, Miriam walked out to the courtyard. Mottele, the goat, was nibbling blades of tender grass in a corner of the yard.

"Oh Mottele! I have to get David out of the orphanage," Miriam said. "I just *have* to! I know they try to make it seem pleasant there, but it's wrong. David needs to be with us, his family. It's just not fair."

Mottele licked her cheek with his raspy tongue. She knew Mottele was just an animal, but he seemed to understand what was in her heart.

Later that night, Miriam played checkers with Grandfather. She picked the red checker from behind his back. They placed their pieces on the board. She concentrated hard on the game. Jump over black, move to the other side to get a king, take off more black pieces.

In the end, he won the game as he always did. "Miriam, you're getting better all the time," Grandfather said as he patted her on the head.

"Thanks, Grandfather. Maybe one day I'll even beat you!"

Everything was starting to make sense. Just as Mottele ate one blade of grass at a time, just as she played checkers one move at a time, so she would make her plan, one step at a time. She would get David out of that orphanage! She would win the game, but this time the prize would be her brother.

CHAPTER 6
Mr. Sharf

David dreamt he was back home. He was playing with the stray kitten. Its claws were digging into his shoulder. He tried to brush them away.

Someone was shaking him.

"Wake up," Joshua whispered.

David wished he could hold fast to the dream. But it vanished like smoke in the sky. He sat up in bed, yawned, and rubbed his eyes. The other boys were fast asleep.

"What's wrong?" David asked.

"Mr. Reznitsky wants to see you."

"Now? What time is it?"

"Past midnight," Joshua said. "You're supposed to come with me."

Shadows, like ghosts, flitted on the wall as David got dressed. The hallway was dimly lit from lamps on the walls. Everything had been going quite well for the last couple of weeks here in the orphanage, just as his grandfather had promised. But suddenly he felt a wave of fear. Something was wrong.

As they walked down the stairs, David whispered. "Why does Mr. Reznitsky want to see me? It's the middle of the night."

Joshua shrugged. "I don't know."

"Am I in trouble?" said David.

"I don't think so, but hurry up," said Joshua. "They're waiting."

"Who?"

"Mr. Reznitsky and another man."

"What other man?"

Joshua only shook his head.

Two men were talking behind the closed door of Mr. Reznitsky's office. Joshua held his finger to his lips as they listened at the door.

"You said this David is the smallest boy here?" said a rasping voice.

"I did," said Mr. Reznitsky.

"Then I want him!" said the voice. "And one more thing."

"Yes?"

"You said the boy has a family?"

"Grandparents and a sister," said Mr. Reznitsky.

David felt tears coming to his eyes.

"Did you arrange with them that he would be taken away?" said the voice.

Mr. Reznitsky paused. "Yes. Of course I did," he said, lying. "But—"

"Don't worry," said the voice. "You'll get your usual payment for this."

Joshua put a hand on David's shoulder and knocked on the door. The sound echoed up and down the hallway.

"Come in," Mr. Reznitsky said. His voice sounded tired and his eyes looked even beadier than usual.

Joshua held the door open and nudged David

forward. He looked at David with pity in his eyes, and then left.

Mr. Reznitsky was sitting behind his desk. He struck a match to his pipe and took a few puffs.

Another man stood in front of Mr. Reznitsky's desk. He was short and had a big belly. His greasy black hair was parted in the middle. He snapped his watch shut and said, "Let's get on with this."

Mr. Reznitsky cleared his throat. "This is David, the boy I told you about."

The stranger stared at David. His black eyes seemed to bore a hole through David's head. Mr. Reznitsky kept looking around the room, at his desk, at the walls, at the floor—anywhere but at David.

"Come now," said the stranger. "Tell the boy."

Mr. Reznitsky took a big breath. "David, this is Mr. Sharf. He owns a weaving factory and—"

"—and I need a small boy to work for me," said Mr. Sharf. "Mr. Reznitsky tells me that you have nimble fingers."

David's heart skipped a beat. "But—"

Mr. Reznitsky was looking down at the ink blotter on his desk and fidgeting with his pipe. "You must go to his factory tonight."

David couldn't move. "Tonight?"

"I have a big order to fill," said Mr. Sharf. "I need you right away."

"You will stay there until the work is done," said Mr. Reznitsky.

David wished Mr. Reznitsky would stop fidgeting and look at him. "Does my grandfather know?" he asked.

"It has all been arranged," said Mr. Reznitsky smoothly. "You will earn some money, which we will send to your grandfather. You would like to help him, wouldn't you?"

"Yes, but—"

"It is settled then," said Mr. Reznitsky. "Time to go." The pipe had gone out. The director waved his hand in dismissal.

David followed Mr. Sharf out the door and down the gravel path to the street. He shivered as the wind blew through his thin jacket. The spring nights were still cold and damp. He pushed his cap down on his head and tried to warm his cold fingers inside his pockets.

A man dozed on the high seat of a wagon, a cigarette dangling from his lips. "Climb up," ordered

Mr. Sharf. "The driver will take you to the factory."
Mr. Sharf turned on his heel, stepped inside a gray
automobile, and drove away.

The driver pointed to the seat beside him, but
David couldn't reach it. Grunting and swearing,
the man pulled David up to the seat. He flicked the
reins and the horse began to move the wagon away
from the orphanage.

David glanced back at the building. *Will I ever
come back here again?* he wondered. *I didn't even
say good-bye to Sam.* He felt a lump in his throat.
Suddenly the orphanage seemed like a haven.

The houses and factories lining the misty streets
looked gray in the early morning light. The damp
air from across the river blew its cold breath on
David's face and neck. He felt frozen in time and
space. *I wish I could wake up from this bad dream,* he
thought. But in his heart, he knew it wasn't a dream.
"We're here, boy," said the driver.

"Where?" asked David. All he could see was the
vague outline of a two-storey brick building. He
tried to rub some warmth into his numb arms and

legs. They didn't feel as if they belonged to his body any longer.

The driver smiled, but it wasn't a real smile. His teeth were broken and yellow; his dirty cap hid his eyes. "Skolna Street." He paused to light another cigarette. "It isn't heaven, that's for sure."

He guided the wagon under a low archway that opened into a wide courtyard. Piles of broken bricks lay in one corner, along with pieces of wood and other debris. David wanted to jump off the wagon and run away. *But where can I go?* he thought.

"Home sweet home," the driver said. He flicked ash from his cigarette onto the ground.

"I told you a hundred times not to smoke here!" shouted an angry voice. A man with a grizzled beard and watery blue eyes limped toward the wagon.

"Take it easy, George," said the driver. "You act like I killed somebody or something." He threw his cigarette down and crushed it with his heel. "The number of cigarettes I've wasted here," he muttered. He pointed with his thumb at David. "The boss said to bring the kid here."

"Kind of small, isn't he?"

The driver shrugged.

"Come here, boy," George said. David scrambled down from the wagon. George turned to the driver and said, "You can go now."

"Glad to be of service," said the driver, smiling his ugly smile. He touched the tip of his cap with a yellow finger. He flicked the reins and drove the wagon out of sight.

"What's your name, boy?" George asked, looking David up and down.

"D…David," he said through chattering teeth. "David…Goldstein."

"Age?"

"Seven."

George narrowed his eyes. "That's all?"

"Almost eight," David whispered.

"The boss should know better," George muttered under his breath.

"What did you say?"

"Nothing," George snapped. "Health?"

"What?"

"Are you healthy?"

Maybe I should lie, David wondered. *Maybe the man will send me back if he thinks I'm sick.*

"Never mind," George said. "We'll find out soon enough." He pushed David forward. "Time to get to work."

CHAPTER 7
The Scavenger

"Move!" said George, shoving David toward the center of an enormous room. The air was filled with dust and fibers. Machines clanged, rattled, and hissed.

"You'll be the scavenger," George shouted, pointing to one of the weaving machines.

"A what?" David asked, coughing.

"You climb under the machine and lie down flat," George said. "When the wheels move to the back, you clean the floor with this." He handed David a small brush.

David gulped. "But…there's not enough space under there for me."

"That's why I said to lie flat." His hard eyes looked at David. "Don't be careless."

"Please! Don't make me get under there!" David pleaded as he backed away.

George grabbed David's arm and slapped him on the face. "Shut up! You'll do what I say or you're out on the street! Now move!"

With all the courage he could muster, David crawled under the whirring machine. Every time it passed over him, his heart beat frantically and sweat poured into his eyes. Over and over the wheels rolled, like a voracious monster. Over and over, David swept up the dust and debris below. He was terrified that he would be crushed by the heavy wheels.

After what seemed like a lifetime, a loud bell rang. The machines slowly ground to a stop.

"Boy, you can come out now," said a woman's voice. "It's time for a break. We have the midday meal now."

David tried to stand up. His arms and legs were stiff. His eyes were burning. His throat was dry.

"Who are you?" he croaked.

"My name is Kalina. And you?" asked the stocky, blond-haired woman.

"David."

"Come with me, David. I'll show you where we eat here in the factory." Kalina looked kindly at David. "You must be careful when you are under there. Last week, the wheels caught the other boy," she whispered. "He lost his arm."

"But—"

"There are no buts here," Kalina said. "You have to pay attention every second." She pointed to a small room with a table and chairs. "Now get in line."

An old woman with two missing fingers ladled beet borscht into a bowl. "Take bread," she grunted. David sat down beside Kalina. He put his head down on his arms and closed his eyes.

"Eat," Kalina said, shaking David on the arm. "You must eat to keep strong."

David raised his head, picked up his heavy spoon, and began to eat.

"Aaron!" Kalina called. "Come over here."

A skinny boy with black hair and brown eyes walked over to where they were sitting. His legs were bent and his back was stooped. He chewed on a piece of bread as he slouched against the table. "What do you want, old woman?" Aaron said, grinning.

"Don't call me that!" said Kalina, wagging her finger at the boy. "Have some respect."

"Sorry. I meant *young* lady," Aaron said, bowing.

"That's better," said Kalina. "This is the new boy. His name is David."

Aaron stared at David. "Poor kid," he said. "What brought you to this hellhole?"

"The driver."

"I didn't say *who*. I said *what*."

David gulped. "They say I'm an orphan."

"Well, are you or aren't you?" Aaron sat down beside David and crossed his arms.

"I guess I am," said David.

Aaron leaned over David's shoulder and reached for his bowl. "If you're not going to eat your soup…"

"Leave him alone," said Kalina, slapping Aaron's hand. "He's got little enough on his bones as it is."

"Hey, I'm doing him a favor," Aaron said. "If he eats too much, he'll get too fat to work under the machine."

David shivered. "Then what?"

Aaron pointed with his thumb toward the door. "Out you go on the street. With not even a piece of bread." He lowered his voice. "Sharf takes little kids like you and kicks them out after he's used them up."

"Don't talk like that," said Kalina.

"It's fine for you," Aaron said. "You're a spinner. You spin the yarn. You're on top of the ladder. I'm an old timer, so I'm a piecer, catching the broken threads and putting them together again." He glanced at David. "But the scavengers are at the very bottom."

Just then, a bell rang.

"Let's go!" said Kalina.

"But I haven't finished eating," David said. Suddenly, he felt very hungry.

"Grab your bread and come! Or George will beat the life out of you!" Kalina said.

David shuddered.

"He likes to use his belt," added Aaron.

David worked until it was dark outside. The constant noise of the machine roared in his ears. While the machine passed over him, David lay flat, as if glued to the floor.

All the while, George walked up and down between the machines. He yelled at the workers and fingered his leather belt. David didn't know if he was more scared of the machine or of George.

When the bell finally rang and the machines had been turned off, David staggered to the table where he forced himself to eat supper—salted herring, boiled potatoes, dark bread, and a glass of tea. After they had finished eating, he followed Aaron up to a room on the second floor of the factory.

"That's your bed," Aaron said, pointing to a cot leaning against a dirty wall. "And don't bother me." He undressed, rolled into bed, and was soon fast asleep.

All night long, bedbugs burrowed out of the cracks in the wall and feasted on David's flesh. He tried to squash the bugs, but they were like an army invading his body. He felt as if he were being eaten alive, one morsel at a time.

David sat at the table after the midday meal the next day. All morning long, he had labored under the terrible machine. Every muscle in his body ached. His eyes stung. His throat was sore. But he knew he couldn't stop for one minute. He had to keep working. There was no choice.

He began to draw a picture of the factory.

"That's pretty good," Aaron said, sitting down beside David. "Where did you learn to draw like that?"

David shrugged. "It doesn't matter," he said.

"Yes, it does. You're good."

"You know," said David, resting his chin on his hand, "I once wanted to be an artist."

"So? Why can't you be one?" Aaron asked.

"I'm just a poor boy." David scratched out his

drawing with vicious strokes. "I wish I could run away from here," he whispered.

"Oh yeah? Where would you run to?"

"I don't know." David shook his head. "If I go back to the orphanage, Mr. Reznitsky will send me back here." He could feel the tears coming to his eyes. "He told Grandfather I'd learn a trade at the orphanage, but—"

"Why did Reznitsky send you here in the first place?"

David rubbed his neck. "I don't know. Maybe... maybe Mr. Sharf is giving him some money."

Aaron whistled. "I wouldn't put it past him," he said. "That Sharf is a crook."

"They promised they would send some money to my family. But now I don't believe them."

"Can you go back home?" Aaron asked.

"No." David held back a sob. "My family can't afford to keep me."

"You'll get used to it here," Aaron said, making a clumsy effort to pat David on the back.

"How long have you been here?" David asked.

"About a year," Aaron said. "But it feels like forever."

"I feel like a mouse in a trap."

Aaron nodded. "Like a mouse in a trap. Without any cheese." He yawned. "I'm going to lie down for a while."

Somewhere people are sitting in a warm room, David thought. *Somewhere people have enough to eat. Somewhere a boy can run home to his family.*

CHAPTER 8
Unexpected Help

That morning, Miriam ate her breakfast, a stale piece of bread, as slowly as she could.

"Finish eating," said Grandmother, hanging up her apron. "You'll be late for work."

Miriam almost gagged when she thought about the butcher shop. Mr. Krangle, the butcher, gave her all the worst jobs. She plucked feathers from the chickens, geese, and ducks. She ground the meat until her arms ached. She swept the floors and wiped the greasy counters. She hated the smell of singed feathers, of blood, of sawdust on the floor.

"And I should go to the market," Grandmother

said. Then she doubled over coughing. When she finally caught her breath, she tied her kerchief under her chin, picked up her basket, and hurried out the door.

Miriam wrapped a few precious pieces of bread in one of Papa's old handkerchiefs, put on her sweater, and closed the door softly behind her. Across the street, she thought she saw David's stray kitten slinking down the alley. The sun shone brightly on the street, making the storefront windows glisten. Miriam felt a warm breeze on her face and heard the rustling of new leaves on the trees.

People trudged along the street. Mothers called to children at play. Students teased each other on the way to school. The milkman drove his skinny horse along the road. The full jugs made a sloshing sound as they jostled in the wagon. The ragman yelled, "Rags to buy! Rags to buy!" The knife-sharpener rang his bell as he pulled his two-wheeled cart behind him.

Miriam walked up to the orphanage. A thin boy was slouched by the gate.

"Excuse me," Miriam said.

"What do you want?" the boy said. "I've got to get to my workshop."

"You don't have to be rude," Miriam said. She hesitated, then looked directly at him. "Wait! Don't I know you? What's your name?"

The boy blushed. "Ben."

"Now I remember! You're the boy with the cookies!"

Ben made a face. "So what?" he said, brushing past her.

"Wait!" said Miriam. "Have you seen my brother, David?"

"He's not here," Ben said.

"Is he in class?" Miriam said.

"He's gone away."

"Gone?" Miriam's heart began to pound. "Where is he?"

Ben hesitated. "I have to go."

"Wait! Please!"

Ben disappeared into the orphanage and closed the door behind him.

Miriam didn't know how long she stood at the gate. Every few minutes she pulled the bell, but no one appeared. It was not visitors' day.

Now she was hungry and thirsty. She remembered the bread she had brought with her. She sank down to the ground. Resting her back against the gate, she untied Papa's handkerchief and chewed on the dry bread. *What should I do now?* she thought. *I can't go back home. I need to find David. If he isn't in the orphanage, where is he?*

She closed her eyes. The morning sun warmed her face.

"Wake up," someone said, shaking her on the shoulder.

"You again?" she said. "What do you want?"

Ben sat down beside her. He took an apple from his pocket and bit into it. "I've decided to help you." He chewed on the apple as if it were the most important thing in the world.

"Help me? But why?" Miriam said.

Ben shrugged. "Why not?" He chewed and swallowed. "Let's say I'm bored. Or maybe I want an adventure. Or maybe—"

"What?"

Ben shook his head. He couldn't admit to this girl that he liked her. There was something about her eyes and her determined chin. He liked the way she had come alone to the orphanage. He wanted to help her. It was a feeling Ben hadn't felt for a long time. He was tired of being disliked by the others in the orphanage. Maybe with this girl, he could have a fresh start.

"Do you want my help or not?" Ben reached into his pocket and handed her another apple. "Here. Bluma won't miss it."

Miriam hesitated, but she was always hungry. "I still don't understand," she said, rubbing the apple on her skirt. "Where is my brother? And how can you help me?" She took a bite and the juice slid down her parched throat.

Ben leaned closer to Miriam. "I know where they took David."

Miriam pulled on Ben's sleeve and said, "Let's go!"

"Not so fast," said Ben. "You can't get him just like that." He snapped his fingers.

"Why not?" said Miriam. "He's my brother."

"You don't know the people who took him. They're very mean and tough." Ben frowned. "They've taken other kids from the orphanage. And the kids don't ever come back."

"What are you talking about?" said Miriam.

"They tell us the kids have been adopted," Ben whispered, "but it's not true." He threw his apple core onto the road.

"So where is he?" pleaded Miriam. "Where's David?"

"In a factory."

"A factory? He's only seven! That's too young to work in a factory," said Miriam. "My teacher said that making young children work in factories is against the law."

Ben snorted. "The owner of *this* factory never had your teacher."

"How did you find out about it?"

Ben smiled. "I have big ears. Besides—"

"What?" said Miriam.

"They tried to take me a while back. But I wouldn't go."

"Why did David go?" Miriam asked.

"They told him if he worked for them, they would give money to your family." Ben shook his head. "But of course they were lying."

"You can't just take a little kid away and make him into a slave!"

"You can come close to it."

"So what should we do?" Miriam said. "How can we get him out of the factory?"

Ben smiled. "Now it's *we*, is it?"

Miriam nodded. Ben leaned closer to Miriam. She could smell apple on his breath.

"I've got a plan," Ben said. "Listen."

CHAPTER 9
At the Restaurant

It was early afternoon when Miriam and Ben reached the factory on Skolna Street. Sunlight glinted on the building's narrow windows. Dirty smoke rose from the chimney. The workers were streaming out through a double door at the side of the building.

"It must be their break time," said Ben.

"What do we do now?" said Miriam.

"Let's wait," Ben said. "Maybe we'll see him." They waited until all the workers had come out, but there was no sign of David.

"Ben?" said Miriam.

"What?"

"I'm hungry."

Ben pointed to the restaurant on the corner. "Come on," he said. "Let's go over there."

"But…" said Miriam. "I can't go in there."

"Why not?"

Miriam blushed. "I don't have any money."

"That's all right," said Ben, jingling some coins in his pocket. "My treat. Come on."

The restaurant was packed with people who came there to eat the main meal of the day. Its walls needed a coat of paint. The wooden tables were scratched with people's initials. But the smell of frying onions wafted in from the kitchen and Miriam's mouth began to water.

Miriam and Ben managed to squeeze in at a table behind some men who were talking loudly. Sausages of various kinds were listed on the menu— blood sausage, pork sausage, garlic sausage—as well as other meat like brains, tripe, liver, and kidneys.

Miriam's stomach turned. She thought she might be sick. "Let's get out of here," she said.

"Why?" asked Ben. "What's wrong?"

"I can't eat this food."

"Why not?"

"It's not kosher," she whispered.

Ben looked at Miriam and burst out laughing.

"Don't laugh at me!" said Miriam. She could feel her face getting red.

"Sorry." Ben was not used to apologizing.

"Let's find another place," Miriam said.

Before they could stand up, a waitress walked over to their table. "Are you here alone?" she asked. "Where are your parents?"

"They…they have to work," Ben said.

"They told us to eat here," said Miriam.

The waitress took out a pad of paper from her apron pocket and licked the lead of her pencil. "Alright. What will it be?"

Ben glanced at Miriam. "Scrambled eggs with onions and potatoes," he said. "But no sausage."

Miriam smiled at Ben. The waitress wrote down the order and walked away.

"I'll be right back," Ben said when they finished eating.

"Where are you going?" asked Miriam. "We have to get back to the factory."

"I have to pay for our food."

"Oh," said Miriam. "Please hurry. We have to find David."

Two women came into the restaurant and sat down near Miriam. One of them began to speak. "Kalina, I'm glad we came here for a change, instead of eating at the factory."

"Me too, Stella."

"The new boy," Stella asked, "what's his name again?"

"David," Kalina said.

Miriam's heart skipped a beat.

"Right. David," said Stella. "Where did he come from?"

"They say he's an orphan. A lot of those young kids who come to work are orphans."

Miriam clenched her fists. *He's not an orphan*, she thought. *Not while he has me.*

"That Mr. Sharf is a real operator," Stella said. "He always finds these little kids and makes them do the most dangerous work."

Miriam gasped. *Who was this Mr. Sharf? And what was the dangerous work he was making David do?*

"There's nothing we can do," said Kalina.

"Nothing," Stella agreed. "We'll lose our lousy jobs if we say anything."

"But it's not right," Kalina said. "I'll try to be nice to him when we go back."

"Let's forget it for now. Where's the waitress?" said Stella. "I'm hungry."

As soon as Ben came back, Miriam told him what she had learned. There wasn't a moment to lose.

At the factory, David had walked over to the lunchroom's dirty window and pressed his nose against the glass. Suddenly, a pebble hit the window from outside. Then another. David peered down at the factory yard. Someone was standing on the far side of the yard. David rubbed his eyes. *It's Miriam!* he thought. *I must be dreaming!*

He saw Miriam bend down to pick up another pebble. A boy was standing beside Miriam. He was bending down to pick up some pebbles, too. He looked familiar. *It's Ben! What is he doing here?* David wondered. *And why is he with Miriam?*

"Look!" said Miriam. "Look at that window!"

"Yeah," said Ben. "I think I see David up there."

Miriam turned toward Ben. "Let's go!"

Ben hesitated. He looked down at the ground. "He might not want to see me."

"Why not?" asked Miriam.

"Let's say, we didn't part on good terms," Ben said.

"What are you talking about?"

"I'll tell you later."

Miriam threw another pebble at the window. She saw David's face, pale as the moon, staring at her. "Look, Ben! It *is* David!"

Suddenly, David disappeared from the window.

Miriam stooped to pick up another pebble and threw it as hard as she could. David did not reappear.

"What happened at the orphanage with you two?" she asked, keeping her eyes on the window.

Ben was glad Miriam wasn't looking at him. "I…I was mean to David," he said.

"You were? But why?"

"I don't know," said Ben.

"You'd better figure it out," said Miriam. "And soon."

"I will," said Ben. He squared his shoulders and glanced at Miriam. "I'll make it up to him," he said. "You'll see."

"Ben, look!" Miriam grabbed Ben's arm. "He's waving at us. Come on!"

"Wait a minute!" Ben whispered. "We can't just storm in there and grab David."

"Why not?"

"We need a plan."

Miriam crossed her arms. "So, go ahead," she said. "Make a plan."

Ben grinned. "Easier said than done." He pulled Miriam's sleeve. "Come on. We'll plan this as we go along."

"My plan exactly," said Miriam.

CHAPTER 10
The Rescue

David saw the two familiar figures run across the yard. Whatever happened, he knew he had to get out of the factory.

He tiptoed toward the outer door of the factory. The sound of his own heart pounded in his ears. He pulled up the latch.

A heavy hand gripped his shoulder. "Where do you think you're going, boy?" a voice growled. David looked up into George's icy eyes.

"I was just—" David mumbled.

"Just what?"

David's shoulder ached from the pressure of the man's hand. "Going to the outhouse."

"Don't give me that!" George grabbed David's arm and pushed him hard. "That's why there's a chamber pot over there in the corner." David tripped and fell backwards. The world began to spin around.

"Leave me alone!" David said, pulling away from George.

"Shut up!" said George. He cuffed David on the ear and yanked him toward the factory floor. "Get back to work!"

David's ears were ringing. He looked over George's shoulder at the door. But George guarded the door with his bulk. David dragged his leaden feet toward the machines. *It's hopeless,* he thought. *I'll never get out of here.*

All at once, the door crashed open. Miriam and Ben rushed in.

"Hey!" George shouted. "What're you kids doing here?"

"David!" Miriam cried.

"Miriam!" David shouted.

Ben pointed at George. "Who's that?" he said.

"The foreman! He won't let me go!" cried David.

"You little brats!" yelled George. "Get out of here if you know what's good for you!" He took out his belt and stepped toward the children.

"Take that!" said Miriam, kicking George in the shins. "For my brother!"

"And that!" said Ben, punching George in the stomach. "For picking on a little kid!"

Miriam ran over to David and grabbed his hand. "Come on!"

"Where?"

"Never mind where," Miriam said. "We've got to get out of here!"

George held Ben's arms behind his back and shook him as if he were a discarded rag on the factory floor. Ben kicked but the man was too strong.

"Come on, David!" Miriam cried. "We have to help Ben!"

"But—"

"No buts!" Miriam grabbed a broom from the corner and pounded George on the back with it.

"What the...?" George growled. He let go of

Ben, and Miriam jumped back. George grabbed her and pressed his hands around her neck, choking her. The broom clattered to the ground.

Just then, David jumped on George's back and put his arms around the man's neck. He hung on with all his strength while Ben kicked George in the shins. George staggered and fell onto the floor.

"Come on!" shouted Ben. "Run!"

The children ran out the door, and Miriam slammed it behind them. The sound echoed up and down the empty street.

They raced along the street and ducked into an alley.

"We did it," panted Ben.

"We sure did," said Miriam, grinning.

"But Miriam," said David. "What do we do now?"

"Miriam has a plan," said Ben.

"No, Ben has a plan," said Miriam.

The children couldn't stop laughing with relief and excitement. They collapsed in a heap behind a row of garbage cans.

CHAPTER 11
Miriam's Plan

"What are you kids doing here?" A bald man with bushy black eyebrows poked them with his broom, as if they were mice hiding in a hole. "You've got no right to be in this alley."

Ben leaped to his feet. "We can stay here as long as we want!"

"No, you can't," said the man, waving his broom at them. "This alley is for tenants only."

Miriam was dirty and exhausted. Her arms throbbed and her throat ached. Her skirt was torn and dirty. *Who do I think I am?* she thought. *How can I keep David safe?* She took a big breath. *No matter what, I have to do everything I can to save my brother.*

"Come on, Ben," Miriam whispered. "Let's get out of here." She stood up and brushed the dust off her skirt.

"Yeah," said David, eying the broom. "Let's go."

"Scat!" shouted the man. "Get out!"

"We're going," said Ben. "You don't have to get so angry."

The janitor waved the broom at them again. "Get out or I'll call the police!"

Ben held his nose and made a face. "It's too smelly here, anyway." They ran out of the alley and scurried along the sidewalk.

"What do we do now?" said David.

"I don't know." Miriam pursed her lips. "Let me think."

"Miriam?" said David.

"What?"

"Do I have to go back to the factory?" David shivered. "It's an awful place. And I don't want to go back to the orphanage. I don't feel safe with Mr. Reznitsky."

Miriam put her hand on David's shoulder and turned him around to face her. "I'll never let you go back to the factory again."

"Never?"

She hugged David fiercely. "Not ever."

"This is a touching scene," said Ben. "But what are we going to do now?"

Miriam took a deep breath. "I know a good hiding place," she said.

"Aren't we going home?" said David. His lips were trembling. "I want to go home."

"No. And not back to the orphanage, either," said Miriam.

"I should be getting back," said Ben.

"Please don't go," Miriam pleaded.

"Tell me where your wonderful hiding place is," Ben said, "and then maybe I'll stay."

Miriam swallowed hard. "In Mottele's shed."

"Who's Mottele?" asked Ben.

"A goat," said David.

"Right, a goat," said Ben, rolling his eyes.

"It's true," said Miriam. "A goat."

"Now I *really* understand," said Ben, shaking his head.

"David needs to hide until people stop looking for him," Miriam said.

"Wait a minute!" said David. "Doesn't anyone know you came for me?"

Miriam looked down at her feet and chewed a fingernail. "Not exactly."

"I'm not moving until you tell me what's going on," said David. He plopped down on the sidewalk. Miriam sat down beside him.

"Fine," said Ben. "I'll be the guard."

"Listen," Miriam said. "I want you to stay in Mottele's shed until I can explain everything to Grandmother and Grandfather." She swallowed hard. "I need to persuade them to let you come home."

"No," David said. "I want to go home *now*."

Suddenly, there was a crash of garbage cans. Cats

began to meow and dogs began to bark. People opened their windows to see what was happening.

"Come on," said Ben. "We've got to get out of here."

The children found a bench on the sidewalk and sat down.

"Please, David," said Miriam. "Just for one night."

"I'll stay with him," Ben offered.

"No way," said David, turning away from Ben. "I remember the mean things you said to me."

Ben looked down at the ground. "I'm sorry, kid," he said.

"Well…" said David. "I don't think I can trust you now."

"David!" said Miriam. "He helped you escape, didn't he?"

"I guess so."

"So, you *have* to trust him," said Miriam. She paused and smiled at Ben. "I do." Ben grinned back at her.

David clenched his jaw. "Well, if you do, then I suppose I do, too."

"Good," said Miriam. "That's settled." She looked at Ben. "How about you, Ben? Don't you have to go back to the orphanage?"

"I can go back any time," said Ben. "The dishes can wait!"

"Thanks, Ben," said Miriam. She leaned over and kissed him on the cheek.

Ben blushed. "Come on," he said. "Show me that famous goat."

CHAPTER 12
Almost Home

Miriam looked up and down Pilsudski Street. "Oh no!"

"What?" said Ben.

"I'm not sure," said Miriam. "Wait. It's—"

"Who?" asked David.

"The police?" said Ben.

"Worse," gasped Miriam. "It's Mrs. Krangle! The butcher's wife. She always sticks her nose into everyone's business. Hide!"

Ben and David quickly turned the corner. Before Miriam could follow them, Mrs. Krangle pounced on her like a cat on a mouse.

"Miriam!" called Mrs. Krangle. "Where were you today? Why didn't you come to work?" She was carrying a brown paper parcel tied with string. Blood had soaked through the bag and was dripping onto the sidewalk. A chicken leg poked through the brown paper. Miriam gagged at the smell.

"I…I wasn't feeling well," Miriam said. "I thought Grandmother told you."

Mrs. Krangle looked Miriam up and down. "She didn't. And why is your blouse so dirty?"

"I tripped and fell," said Miriam.

"Humph," said Mrs. Krangle, pressing her lips together. She squinted at Miriam. "Will you be at work tomorrow? There are plenty of other girls—"

"I will, Mrs. Krangle," said Miriam. "I'm sorry."

"All right then," said Mrs. Krangle. "I'll see you tomorrow."

"Good-bye," said Miriam.

"Good-bye," said Mrs. Krangle. A trail of chicken blood followed her down the street.

"Whew! That was close," said Ben.

David pinched his nose. "She's *so* smelly!"

"That's the chicken," said Miriam. She looked over her shoulder. "We've got to go."

The children dashed from the shadow of one building to another. At last they reached home. They hid behind the garbage cans in the courtyard at the back of the building.

"I'm getting tired of smelling garbage," Ben said.

"Me too!" said David.

In the yard, Mottele was champing grass near the outhouse.

"It's locked," said Miriam, rattling the door of the shed.

"Don't worry," said Ben. "I can handle this." He took a small knife out of his pocket, pushed Miriam out of the way, and began to pick at the lock.

"Where did you learn to do that?" asked David.

Ben pressed his lips together. "Quiet! I need to concentrate."

Miriam stood behind David, her hands on his shoulders. Her heart was beating so loudly she was sure Grandmother or Grandfather could hear it from inside the building. She heard a faint click.

Ben held up the opened lock. "Like magic!" he announced.

"It stinks in here!" David cried as he peeked inside. "Goat droppings! No way am I staying here!"

Faint light from the setting sun leaked in through the grimy window and shone on spider webs attached to every corner. A thin layer of dirty straw lay on the dusty floor. An old mattress was shoved against one wall.

"It's not so bad," Miriam said. "Look. There's even a mattress here."

David crossed his arms. "It's disgusting inside! I'm not staying!"

"David, you need to sleep here tonight," said Miriam. "I'll come get you in the morning."

"I don't want to!" David's voice was shaking. "I hate spiders! And I'm scared to be alone."

"I told you," said Ben. "I'll stay here with you."

"You really will?" David groped in his pocket and pulled out his crumpled handkerchief. He blew his nose loudly and stuffed the handkerchief back into his pocket.

"Try the mattress," suggested Miriam. She found a potato sack in the corner and shook out the dust. "Lie down and before you know it, it will be morning."

David yawned. "And you'll come get me then?"

"I promise," said Miriam.

David yawned again. "Ben? You'll stay here with me?"

Ben nodded.

"All right," David mumbled. "Watch out for the spiders."

"I will," said Ben.

David curled up in a ball and closed his eyes.

"Go now," whispered Ben. "I'll take care of him."

Miriam began to leave, but then turned back. "Ben, thanks for everything."

CHAPTER 13
Miriam in Trouble

Miriam slinked along the alley, turned the corner, and bumped right into her grandmother. Mrs. Krangle followed her, still carrying the bloody parcel under her arm.

"Miriam! Where have you been?" Grandmother grabbed Miriam by the shoulders. "Where did you go? I've been worried sick!" She put her hands on her hips. "Tell me right now." Her kerchief was askew and a corner of her shawl was dragging on the ground.

"I told you I saw her," said Mrs. Krangle.

"I…" Miriam mumbled and looked down at her feet.

"Tell your grandmother," said Mrs. Krangle.

"You were supposed to go to work," said Grandmother. She raised her hand but then lowered it. "Where were you? Tell me right now. And don't lie to me again."

"Tell her," said Mrs. Krangle.

"Mrs. Krangle," Grandmother said, "This is between me and my granddaughter." She raised her chin and wrapped her shawl around her shoulders.

"I was only trying to help," said Mrs. Krangle.

"Mrs. Krangle, it is time for you to go," said Grandmother evenly.

"All right. I'm going," said Mrs. Krangle as she turned and walked away.

"Now talk," said Grandmother.

Miriam stared at the cracks in the sidewalk. "I'm sorry, Grandmother," she said. "I had to do something."

"What do you mean, *do* something?" Grandmother cried. "I was so worried about you!" She pushed Miriam forward. "Go inside right now."

When they entered the room, Grandmother sighed, hugged Miriam, and said, "Are you hungry?"

Miriam shook her head.

"Then go to bed." Grandmother sighed again. "I'll join you soon. Your grandfather will be home in a while. I'll tell him you are safe. We'll talk about this tomorrow."

How can I explain? thought Miriam, sinking down on the bed she shared with her grandmother. *They'll never understand. I went to the orphanage, kidnapped David from the factory, and hid him away. For any of those things, I'll be punished. For all of those things, they'll probably never talk to me again.* Miriam's heart skipped a beat. *Maybe they'll be so angry, they'll send me away, too.*

Miriam woke to the sound of chirping birds and the call of the water-carrier, "Water! Water! Who wants water today?" The warm sun streamed in through the window.

Grandmother walked over to the bed and sat down beside her. "Grandfather had to go out. Now tell me," she said. "Where did you go yesterday? What did you do?"

Miriam didn't answer. She wanted to tell Grandmother the truth, but she couldn't. Not yet. "I wanted to take a day off work," she said. "That's all."

Grandmother pressed her lips together. "I don't understand why you didn't tell me," she said.

"I'm sorry," Miriam mumbled.

"Will you go to work today and make no more trouble?"

"Yes, Grandmother."

"I have to take my sweaters to the market." She paused. "Can I trust you?"

Miriam nodded.

"All right then." Grandmother tightened her kerchief, picked up her basket, and with one glance over her shoulder, closed the door.

After Grandmother left, Miriam got dressed. She took a piece of bread for herself and wrapped two more pieces in a newspaper for David and Ben. As she approached the shed in the courtyard, she whispered, "David. Ben." She opened the door. Except for a few spiders scurrying out of sight, the shed was empty. The boys were gone.

Miriam plopped down on the ground in front of the shed. Tears streamed down her cheeks. *Where could David have gone?* she wondered. *And where is Ben?*

She didn't feel brave anymore. With all her heart, she wished Mama and Papa were still alive. She wished—oh, so much!

Miriam felt Mottele's rasping tongue licking the tears on her face. She stroked his neck. She unwrapped a piece of bread and gave it to Mottele while she ate the other piece. As she chewed, her head swam with wild imaginings. *Maybe some robbers came in the middle of the night and kidnapped David! By now, he might be in the big city: Krakow or Lodz or even Warsaw!*

Miriam stood up, shook the crumbs off her skirt, and walked slowly out of the courtyard. *My plan failed,* she thought. *All I wanted was to make everything better. But all I've done is make everything worse.*

She went to work, but the hours passed in a blur. She did her tasks without thinking and wasn't even bothered by the smells. She couldn't stop worrying about what had happened to David and Ben. She was afraid to tell Grandmother and Grandfather. At the same time, she was afraid not to.

That night, Miriam couldn't fall asleep. She could hear distant noises. A trolley car squealed on its tracks. A drunken man sang as he staggered home from the tavern. Suddenly, she heard a sound right under the window. She crept out of bed and looked outside.

Ben was standing on the pavement, waving his arms at her. With trembling fingers, Miriam slipped her coat over her nightgown.

"Where are you going?" murmured Grandmother from the other side of the bed.

"To the outhouse," Miriam said.

"All right." Grandmother rolled over and began to snore.

"What are you doing here?" Miriam whispered

when she reached Ben. "And where's David?" She shivered. The damp air was filled with coal smoke from thousands of chimneys.

"We can't talk here," said Ben. "Someone might see us."

Miriam followed Ben along the side of the building until they reached the courtyard.

"Talk," Miriam said, crossing her arms. "This better be good."

Ben cleared his throat. "After you left," he began, "David and I started talking."

"And?"

"And we decided that your plan wouldn't work."

"Oh? And I suppose you have a better plan?"

Ben grinned. "As a matter of fact, we do." He drew himself up to his full height. "Can you come to the orphanage first thing in the morning?"

Miriam bit her lip. "I don't know," she said. "I'm in big trouble already."

"You've got to," Ben insisted. "We need your help." He leaned over and whispered in Miriam's ear. "Here's what you have to do."

CHAPTER 14
The Truth About Mr. Reznitsky

When Miriam arrived at the orphanage the next morning, Ben was standing near the gate. He led her to the storeroom where David was waiting for them.

"David!" Miriam cried as she hugged her brother. "I was worried about you. Are you all right?"

"Of course I am," said David.

"Where were you?" asked Miriam. "Where did you go? And what did you eat?"

"We've been fine," said David.

"We stayed with some older kids who used to be in the orphanage," Ben said. "I told you I'd take care of your brother."

"And he did, too," said David.

"Thank you," said Miriam. She could feel the tears welling up in her eyes.

"We've got to get going," said Ben. "Is everyone ready?"

The other two nodded.

"Let's go."

David opened the door. Then, as Miriam and Ben snuck down the corridor, he closed the door softly behind him and hid in the storeroom.

A few minutes later, the fire alarm bell began to ring. Miriam let out her breath. David had done his part in their plan. She heard people shouting and doors opening and closing. Miriam and Ben crept toward Mr. Reznitsky's office.

"You know what to do," Ben said to Miriam. "I'll guard the door while you go inside."

Miriam nodded. She turned the handle of the office door. "Ben," she whispered. "It's locked!"

"Leave it to me." He reached into his pants pocket and took out a small metal tool. Again, Ben skillfully managed to pick the lock.

Mr. Reznitsky's office looked the same as it had the first time she had gone there. Books stood on shelves. The children's artwork was still tacked to the board. The canary still sat on its perch.

Miriam took down David's drawing. She folded it and tucked it into her pocket.

Next Miriam searched Mr. Reznitsky's desk. She opened the top drawer. It held supplies such as pencils, rubber bands, and paper clips. Envelopes with bills and receipts filled the middle drawer. The bottom one contained a bottle of vodka, two glasses, and a can of pipe tobacco.

She pulled on the narrow drawer at the front. It was locked. She remembered seeing a small key in the top drawer. With shaking fingers, she picked up the key and turned it in the lock. It opened with a satisfying click.

Miriam rummaged through the letters and envelopes inside the drawer. Among them was a letter from Mr. Sharf. She had almost finished reading it when she heard voices in the hallway outside the office. She quickly locked the drawer again, put the key back, and tucked the letter into her pocket next to David's drawing.

"Mr. Reznitsky!" Ben called outside the door.

Miriam tiptoed to the door to hear what was going on.

"Yes? What is it?" Mr. Reznitsky asked. "I have to call the police. Someone pulled a false alarm."

"I think I know who did it."

"You do?"

"Come with me, sir," said Ben. "I'll take you to him."

"All right," said Mr. Reznitsky. "But make it quick. I'm expecting a visitor."

A few moments later, someone knocked on the office door. When there was no answer, he began to turn the doorknob. Miriam retreated behind the long curtains for cover.

A distinguished-looking man with a cane entered the room. Wisps of white hair peeked out from under his fedora hat. The man sat down on Mr. Reznitsky's leather chair and took out a pocket watch. Behind the curtains, Miriam's heart was pounding and her hands were sweating. She tried to shrink back into the shadows. Then she sneezed.

The man stood up and raised his cane. "Who are you?" he asked. "And what are you doing here?"

Miriam stepped forward. She swallowed hard. "My name is Miriam Goldstein," she said in a shaking voice. "My brother, David, came here two weeks ago."

The man raised his eyebrows. "And what, may I ask, are you doing in Mr. Reznitsky's office?" Miriam looked down at her feet. "Young lady," the man said. "Sit down."

With shaking legs, Miriam sat down facing the man.

"My name is Mr. Perlman," he said. "I am on the Orphanage Committee which runs this place." He stroked his short mustache and looked kindly at Miriam. "Now please explain what you are doing here."

Miriam took the paper from her pocket and handed it to him. "I…I found this in Mr. Reznitsky's desk. You need to read this."

Mr. Perlman unfolded it and said, "But this isn't a letter. It's a drawing!"

"Oh, sorry," said Miriam. She took out the letter from her pocket. "Here it is."

As Mr. Perlman read the letter, his eyebrows drew together, forming one line. When he had finished reading, he folded the letter and tucked it into his jacket pocket.

"Now I understand," he said, as if talking to himself. "For a long time, we have been wondering how Mr. Reznitsky could afford such a nice house and a fancy car on the salary we pay him." He held out his hands. "Which isn't enough, goodness knows."

Mr. Perlman looked sharply at Miriam. "Young lady?"

"Yes?" Miriam was glad she was sitting down, for her legs were still trembling.

"Did you find anything else when you were *accidentally* looking in Mr. Reznitsky's desk?"

Miriam shook her head. "No, Mr. Perlman."

He stroked his mustache again. "Our committee is responsible for the welfare of the children here."

He paused. "This letter proves Mr. Reznitsky took money for work that children were forced to do in Sharf's factory." He looked at Miriam. "Do you have anything else to say?"

"No except—"

"Except?"

"Except I'm sorry I went through Mr. Reznitsky's desk." Miriam looked down at the floor, chewing her fingernail. She gazed into Mr. Perlman's eyes. "I know it's not right, but I just *had* to prove what Mr. Reznitsky was doing!"

Mr. Perlman nodded. "Sometimes a person must do something wrong in order to correct a bigger wrong." He paused. "I will take this letter to the other committee members immediately. We will straighten this matter out."

Miriam breathed a sigh of relief.

"And now, Miriam Goldstein," said Mr. Perlman, standing up.

"Yes?"

"Don't you think it is time to go?"

Miriam crept along the corridor, walked out the

front door, and hurried down the path to the gate. When she was out of sight of the orphanage at last, she ran until she came to the butcher shop.

"Where have you been?" Mrs. Krangle demanded.

Miriam sighed. "It's a long story."

CHAPTER 15
The End Is the Beginning

Everyone sat around the table after the Friday night meal. Mr. Perlman had given Ben permission to leave the orphanage for the Sabbath.

Grandfather looked sternly at Miriam. "It's time to explain what's been going on," he said. "Mr. Perlman told me part of the story, but I want to hear it from you children."

Miriam blushed and looked down at the floor. She took a deep breath. "I helped David escape from the factory."

Grandfather nodded. "And then what did you do?"

"I...I broke into Mr. Reznitsky's office and stole a letter from his desk."

"She had to prove what he was doing!" said Ben.

"She was only trying to help!" said David.

"You children should not have taken matters into your own hands," said Grandfather.

"It was foolish," said Grandmother, wagging her finger at them.

"We had to," said Miriam. "No one else would do anything!"

Grandfather continued. "Mr. Perlman called an emergency meeting of the Orphanage Committee this afternoon."

"What happened?" Miriam and Ben asked at the same time.

Grandfather smiled. "Mr. Reznitsky has been fired."

"Hurray!" the children shouted.

"What happened to Mr. Sharf?" asked David.

"The police arrested him," said Grandfather.

"Hurray!" the children shouted again.

"They're going to charge him with illegal child

labor," explained Grandfather.

Everyone began to talk at once, until Grandfather shouted, "Quiet!"

"Can David stay home now?" Miriam asked.

The grownups were silent.

"And what about Ben?" Miriam asked.

"I'll be all right," Ben said. "Who knows? Maybe I'll go to trade school." He grinned. "I could become a locksmith."

"Young man," said Grandfather, putting his hand on Ben's shoulder. "How would you like to become my apprentice? You could help me with the work my poor fingers can no longer do."

Ben stared at Grandfather. "You…you would teach me to be a real locksmith?" he said.

"You have a definite talent in that direction," Miriam said. Ben smiled and bowed at Miriam.

"I think you'll make a fine locksmith," Grandfather said. "Besides, I'll need your help. Mr. Perlman said he'll find more work for me. He said that's the least he can do because of what happened to David."

"Then I'll become your apprentice," said Ben. His eyes were shining. "Thank you."

"So what about me?" said David.

"You," said Grandmother, pointing at David. "You are a boy who makes trouble."

"But one who is very brave," said Grandfather.

David beamed, but then his face fell. "But…will I have to go back to the orphanage?"

"Come here, you young scamp," said Grandfather. He ruffled David's hair. "With Ben to help me, and Miriam working at the butcher shop—"

Miriam made a face.

"—we will be able to manage."

"Then I can stay home?" asked David.

Grandmother wiped her tears with her shawl and hugged David. "Yes, dear boy, you can stay home."

"Hurray!" the children shouted again.

When the yelling had died down, Grandmother said, "Miriam, if it weren't for you, we might have lost David. We are very grateful."

Miriam felt a lump in her throat.

"But if you ever lie to me again…" Grandmother started to say.

"I won't," said Miriam. "I promise. But—"

"What?" Grandmother and Grandfather asked at the same time.

"Will I be able to go back to school some day?" She held her breath.

"Let's wait and see what happens in the fall," Grandmother said.

Miriam breathed a sigh of relief. Fall was a long time away. Anything might happen between now and then.

"Now that everything is settled," said Grandfather, "let's have a glass of tea." He winked at Grandmother. "And maybe a cookie?"

"Grandfather?" said Miriam.

Grandfather raised his eyebrows. "Yes?"

"You owe me a game of checkers." Miriam smiled. "And maybe this time, I'll win."

AFTERWORD FROM THE AUTHOR

The Orphan Rescue is based on a family story that my father told me many years ago. While some of it is true, I wrote the book inspired by the events of the time and because the experiences of the characters are relevant to young people now.

The true story is that David, whose real name was Alter Chaim, lived at the Jewish Orphanage in Sosnowiec. And he did have a sister named Miriam. Poverty forced their family to place Alter Chaim in the orphanage.

Decades later, such extreme poverty still forces parents in many parts of the world to give up their children. Today it is more often girls who are compelled to leave their families. Some are sent far away from home and may never return.

Like David in the story, other children today are forced to work in places such as factories and mills, mines and quarries, hotels and restaurants, on farms and in homes as servants. Their parents cannot afford proper food, clothing, and shelter, so instead of going to school, these very young boys and girls work to help support their families.

I don't think anyone should have to live like that today. Do you?

This book is dedicated to my cousins, Miriam and Alter Chaim, and to all children today who deserve a better future.

ACKNOWLEDGMENTS

My beloved father, Morris Dublin, gave me the idea for this book and shared his memories of life in Sosnowiec before World War II.

Ann Kirschner, author of *Sala's Gift*, kindly offered insight about life in Sosnowiec in the 1930s.

Rabbi Dow Marmur, rabbi emeritus of Holy Blossom Temple, Toronto, was a young child in Sosnowiec. He carefully read an early draft of this book and generously offered very helpful suggestions.

Claire Goldstein Simmons led our Jewish heritage tour (2007) through Poland and the Czech Republic with wisdom and passion.

Dr. Artur Szyndler, director of education and research at the Auschwitz Jewish Center, guided me through Sosnowiec; Waclaw Wojciechowski, through Jewish sites in Poland. They generously shared their knowledge with me.

My writers' group offered constructive comments for every chapter: Rona Arato, Sydell Waxman, Lynn Westerhout, and Frieda Wishinsky. They are not only my fellow writers but also my dear friends.

Others who helped along the way: Meryl Arbing, Bambi Katz, Mark Mazer, Myrna Ross, and Judy Saul.

At Second Story Press: Margie Wolfe, publisher, challenged me to make this the best book it could be; Carolyn Jackson led me through the editing process with her usual unassuming expertise; Sarah Swartz, editor, gave me the courage to use a large pair of virtual scissors; Melissa Kaita proved her patience and artistry once again; Emma Rodgers welcomed all my suggestions for marketing; Qin Leng, through her skilful illustrations, brought to life what I had previously held only in my heart and imagination.

ANNE DUBLIN is an award-winning author of books for young readers. She lives in Toronto.

To find out more visit her website:
www.annedublin.ca

DATE DUE